Head and Shoulders

Retold by MEGAN BORGERT-SPANIOL

Illustrated by DAN CRISP

CANTATA
LEARNING

MANKATO, MINNESOTA

CANTATA LEARNING

MANKATO, MINNESOTA

Published by Cantata Learning
1710 Roe Crest Drive
North Mankato, MN 56003
www.cantatalearning.com

Library of Congress Control Number: 2014938299
ISBN: 978-1-63290-060-9

Head and Shoulders retold by Megan Borgert-Spaniol
Illustrated by Dan Crisp

Book design by Tim Palin Creative
Music produced by Wes Schuck
Audio recorded, mixed, and mastered at Two Fish Studios, Mankato, MN

Printed in the United States of America.

VISIT

WWW.CANTATALEARNING.COM/ACCESS-OUR-MUSIC

Our body parts work together so that we can move in all kinds of ways. They let us write our names, ride bikes, eat food, and give hugs. They also let us smile, **shrug**, and shout. Think of all of the things that you can do with each body part in this song!

When you hear the chime, turn the page.

Head, shoulders, knees and toes,
knees and toes.
Head, shoulders, knees and toes,
knees and toes.

And eyes and ears and mouth and nose.
Head, shoulders, knees and toes,
knees and toes.

Feet, tummy, arms and chin,
arms and chin.

Feet, tummy, arms and chin,
arms and chin.

And eyes and ears and mouth and **shin**.

Feet, tummy, arms and chin,

arms and chin.

Head, shoulders, knees and toes,
knees and toes.
Head, shoulders, knees and toes,
knees and toes.

And eyes and ears and mouth and nose.

Head, shoulders, knees and toes,

knees and toes.

Hands, fingers, legs and lips,

legs and lips.

Hands, fingers, legs and lips,

legs and lips.

And eyes and ears and mouth and **hips**.

Hands, fingers, legs and lips,

legs and lips.

Head, shoulders, knees and toes,

knees and toes.

Head, shoulders, knees and toes,

knees and toes.

And eyes and ears and mouth and nose.

Head, shoulders, knees and toes,

knees and toes.

Cheeks, forehead, wrists and gums,

wrists and gums.

Cheeks, forehead, wrists and gums,

wrists and gums.

And eyes and ears and mouth and thumbs.

Cheeks, forehead, wrists and gums,

wrists and gums.

Head, shoulders, knees and toes,

knees and toes.

Head, shoulders, knees and toes,

knees and toes.

And eyes and ears and mouth and nose.

Head, shoulders, knees and toes,

knees and toes.

Head, shoulders, knees and toes,

knees and toes.

Head, shoulders, knees and toes,

knees and toes.

And eyes and ears and mouth and nose.

Head, shoulders, knees and toes,

knees and toes.

Head, shoulders, knees and toes.

21

GLOSSARY

gums—the soft pink tissue that surrounds the teeth

hips—the large, rounded bones below the waist and above the legs

shin—the part of the leg below the knee

shrug—to move your shoulders up and back down

Head and Shoulders

Public Domain
Polka

Head shoul - ders knees and toes knees and toes.

Head shoul - ders knees and toes knees and toes. And

eyes and ears and mouth.......... and............ nose,

head shoul - ders knees and toes knees and toes.

TO LEARN MORE

Arnold, Tedd. *Parts*. New York: Dial Books for Young Readers, 1997.

Clark, Katie. *A Tour of Your Muscular and Skeletal Systems*. North Mankato, MN: Capstone Press, 2013.

Lindeen, Carol. *My Bones*. Mankato, MN: Capstone Press, 2007.

Rabe, Tish. *Inside Your Outside!* New York: Random House, 2003.

Rau, Dana Meachen. *Look!: A Book About Sight*. Minneapolis: Picture Window Books, 2005.